TO THE RESCUE

FLASH FLOOD

SCHOLASTIC INC.
New York   Toronto   London   Auckland   Sydney
Mexico City   New Delhi   Hong Kong   Buenos Aires

The author would like to thank Timothy Cohn
of the United States Geological Survey
for his expert advice in preparing this manuscript.

Written by Anne Capeci.

Illustrations by Steve Haefele.

Based on *The Magic School Bus* books
written by Joanna Cole and illustrated by Bruce Degen.

ISBN 0-439-42941-2

12 11 10 9 8 7 6 5 4 3 2 1   3/0   4/0   5/0   6/0   7/0

Designed by Peter Koblish

Printed in the U.S.A.   40

First printing, March 2003

INTRODUCTION

My name is Dorothy Ann — D.A. for short. I am one of the kids in Ms. Frizzle's class.

Maybe you have heard of Ms. Frizzle. (Sometimes we just call her the Friz.) She is a terrific teacher — but strange. One of her favorite subjects is science, and she knows everything about it. I love science, too.

She takes us on lots of field trips on the Magic School Bus. Believe me, it's not called *magic* for nothing! We never know what's going to happen when we get on that bus.

Ms. Frizzle likes to surprise us, but we can usually tell when she is planning a special lesson — we just look at what she's wearing.

One day, Ms. Frizzle showed up wearing this outfit. As soon as I saw her, I knew we were going to be in for a wet and wild adventure! Let me tell you all about it. . . .

CHAPTER 1

"I can't believe it's raining *again*," said Phoebe.

"We've had wet weather for weeks!" Tim said.

All the kids in Ms. Frizzle's class were tromping in to start the day. Actually, it was more like we were *swimming* in. Every single one of us was soaked from coming to school in the pouring rain. Water dripped from our slickers and rain boots and made puddles on the floor.

"This must be the rainiest spring on record," Ralphie said. He squeezed water from

his baseball cap and turned to me. "Don't you think so, D.A.?"

I wasn't surprised that he asked *me* that question. After all, I *am* the biggest science expert in our class. I'm always reading up on our latest topic.

"This is the most rain we've had in 15 years," I said. "I heard on the news that if it keeps up, the rivers and streams in our area could flood."

Just then, Ms. Frizzle came in. She was singing to herself. Liz, the class lizard, was on her shoulder. They were both dripping wet, but neither of them seemed to mind.

"Good morning, class!" Ms. Frizzle greeted us. "Isn't it a glorious day? There's lovely liquid as far as the eye can see!"

Okay. Maybe the Friz *does* have an unusual way of looking at things. That's one of the things we love about her!

Well, most of us, anyway.

"You call this glorious?" Arnold gulped, looking nervously out the window. "D.A. just finished telling us it could flood!"

From the Desk of Ms. Frizzle

Water: It's Not Always Wet!

Water can exist in three forms:
1. Solid (like snow and ice)
2. Liquid (like rain and lakes)
3. Gas (water vapor in the air)

Liquid

Solid

Gas (You can't see water vapor!)

"Rain is a normal part of the water cycle, Arnold," Ms. Frizzle said. "That includes heavy rains like the ones we've been having."

Everyone nodded — even Arnold. After all, we had just finished studying the water cycle. Our whole class had worked together to make a big poster that hung on the wall.

Where Water Goes

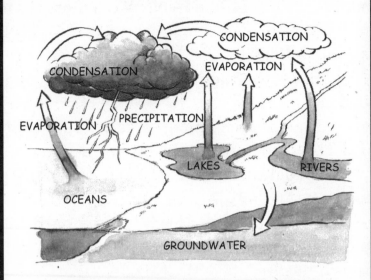

Water is always on the move. Water in oceans, lakes, and rivers *evaporates* (changes from a liquid to a gas). Plants release water vapor through their leaves in a process called transpiration. The water in the air then forms clouds and falls back to the earth as rain, ice, or snow. It seeps into the ground or flows into rivers, lakes, and streams. Then the sun heats the water up, and the process starts all over again!

Wanda looked at the chart, then frowned at the growing puddles on the grass outside. "This still doesn't seem normal to me," she said. "The whole school yard is turning into a lake!"

"Some weather *is* extreme," the Friz admitted.

"Like that summer a few years ago," said Tim, "when it hardly ever rained and we had a drought. My mom's whole garden dried up."

"Droughts *and* floods cause hardship and damage, but they also play an important part in nature," said Ms. Frizzle.

"You mean a *destructive* part," Keesha said. "A flooding river could wreck houses and hurt people. That's not normal. It's *scary.*"

All of a sudden Ms. Frizzle got "the look" — a special sparkle that comes into her eyes whenever she has something far-out in mind for us.

"It's time we *soaked* up a few facts on floods ourselves. Don't you fret, we can't learn about floods without getting wet!" she an-nounced. "To the bus, class!"

Some kids didn't look thrilled to go back out in the pouring rain. But I ran to get my backpack and rain slicker right away. What can I say? I want to be a scientist, and field trips on the Magic School Bus are the most amazing way to do research!

I couldn't wait to see what kind of ad-venture the Friz would get us into this time.

CHAPTER 2

Soon we were all buckled up, and Ms. Frizzle hit the gas.

"We're on our way!" she said.

Instead of going forward, we went up. Straight up. The Magic School Bus twirled around as it rose into the air!

"It's up, up, and away," said Ralphie. "Right to the clouds!"

As the bus went higher, it got smaller, too. Soon it was smaller than the raindrops falling all around us. We were so tiny that those drops looked like gigantic water balloons! Every time a drop went by the bus, it felt like an earthquake.

"Every flood starts with lots and lots of lovely precipitation," Ms. Frizzle told us.

A Word from Tim

Precipitation is water that falls from clouds as rain, sleet, snow, or hail.

"I guess if there's enough rain," Carlos said, "people can really get in over their heads."

Carlos always makes the silliest jokes. He can't stop himself! But I guess I'm kind of the same way when it comes to spreading the word about science.

I reached into my backpack and pulled out a book I had checked out of the library. "It says in here that heavy rains and melting snow are the biggest causes of river floods," I told everyone.

"But when so much of the rain and snow falls on land," Phoebe said, "how does that make *rivers* overflow?"

Name That Flood
by Carlos

River floods are just one kind of flood. Here are some others:

• Coastal floods take place when storm winds pile up ocean water and make it surge onto land.

• Flash floods usually happen along small streams and in mountainous areas. Why are flash floods so dangerous? Because they happen so fast that people can't get out of harm's way. During a drenching rain, streambeds or gullies can overflow in minutes — or even seconds.

Phoebe had a good point. When we looked out the windows, we didn't see any streams or rivers below us. There was just a big, grassy, wet hillside surrounded by woods.

"Excellent question, Phoebe!" said the

Friz. "Luckily we're in exactly the right place to learn the answer."

Ms. Frizzle steered the Magic School Bus beneath a fat raindrop and —

Splat!

The raindrop fell right onto the bus. It completely surrounded us! I was really glad the windows were shut.

All of a sudden, we weren't going up anymore. We fell down, down, down inside the raindrop.

"Look out below!" Carlos shouted.

"Wow!" I said, writing down some observations in my notebook. "So *this* is what it's like to be a raindrop."

The hillside below was coming up fast. Before we knew it, our raindrop splattered onto the wet grass.

"Whoa!" Phoebe cried.

The bus bounced a few times. Luckily, landings on the Magic School Bus are always *magically* safe, and everyone was fine.

"I still don't see any river or lake — or any kind of water that could flood," Tim said.

"Precipitation that falls on land can still reach rivers, lakes, and oceans," Ms. Frizzle told us. "Sometimes it even travels underground."

Going Down
by Ralphie

The earth's soil is like a sponge that soaks up rain. Gravity pulls the rainwater down until it eventually reaches the water table. That's where the spaces in rocks and soil begin to be completely filled with water. All the water below the water table is called groundwater.

"I get it," Wanda said. "Even if the ground is dry, there is water beneath the surface."

Carlos nodded. "And the water table *serves up* groundwater to rivers, lakes, and springs," he added with a laugh.

From the Desk of Ms. Frizzle

Groundwater travels underground. Wherever it meets the surface of the land, it can bubble up in a spring or flow into a lake, a stream, or the ocean. Thanks to groundwater, bodies of water, wetlands, and wells can get water even when the weather is dry.

"Wait a minute. This soil is already totally soaked," I pointed out. "See how most of the water is pooling up on top of the ground? There's no way it can absorb much more rain."

At that moment, the bus lurched and shifted. The pooled-up rain was starting to stream down the hillside — and it was taking us along for the ride!

Runaway Runoff
by Arnold

When water from precipitation falls to the ground, some of it seeps into the soil or is soaked up by plants. Some evaporates. The rest flows on top of the land to streams and other bodies of water. Water that travels on top of the ground is called surface runoff. About 30 percent of all precipitation is runoff. That's a lot of runaway water!

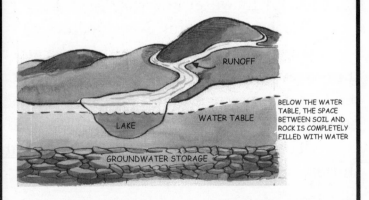

RUNOFF

BELOW THE WATER TABLE, THE SPACE BETWEEN SOIL AND ROCK IS COMPLETELY FILLED WITH WATER

WATER TABLE

LAKE

GROUNDWATER STORAGE

"The teachers at my old school never let us get washed away," Phoebe said.

"Isn't it marvelous?" Ms. Frizzle grinned from ear to ear. "Gravity is doing a wonderful job of pulling this runoff downhill toward the closest stream."

"Runoff really knows how to bring you down," said Carlos.

"Carlos!" we all groaned.

But he was right. The runoff *was* taking the Magic School Bus down — right down the grassy hillside and into the woods. Talk about a wet and wild way to do research! We were so small that floating on that rivulet was like being tossed around on a huge river. (Just so you know, a rivulet is a small stream.) For a while, all we saw was water and woods. And then . . .

"There's a stream!" Keesha said.

Our runoff was flowing toward a stream that went through the woods. That stream might have seemed small to a regular-sized person. To us, it was like a raging ocean.

"This runoff is going to dump us right in there!" said Wanda.

"Great!" I said.

Everyone looked at me as if I were totally crazy.

"According to my research, that's exactly what runoff is *supposed* to do," I explained. "At least we're not alone. There's lots of *other* runoff, too."

Hundreds of rivulets of rainwater drained into the stream from the land all around.

There was so much water that the stream almost reached the tops of its banks. Was it ever moving fast! The water was white and foamy.

"Right you are, D.A.!" the Friz said. "Runoff from all over the woods is pouring into the stream."

Floating in the swollen, rushing stream was really exciting. I could tell Arnold was scared, but I liked seeing all that water and thinking about where it would go next.

Wet, Wet, Wet!
by Keesha

When an area of land gets too wet the land needs to shed, or get rid of, the excess water. The water heads downhill toward the closest stream or river. A watershed is the area of land that drains into a single river or stream. A watershed can be as small as a few acres or as large as many hundreds of thousands of square miles.

"I bet the stream will flow into a bigger river downstream," I said. "Or maybe even into a lake or an ocean!"

Ralphie's brow furrowed beneath his baseball cap. "Does that mean all this rushing water will make the river flow faster and higher farther down?" he asked.

"Absolutely!" the Friz told him. "Heavy rains *up*river can cause floods *down*river."

The racing water was really noisy. Rushing water echoed all around us. Then we heard a rumbling inside the bus. It came from Liz's stomach!

"Um, Ms. Frizzle? I think Liz is hungry!" said Phoebe.

The Friz pulled a box of Lucky Lizard Lumps from the glove compartment. She opened it, and a smell filled the bus. It was like . . . like . . . well, I can't think of *any* smell quite like it. I guess you could just say it smelled weird — like Lucky Lizard Lumps!

Liz took one whiff and her stomach growled even louder. But when Ms. Frizzle opened the box, it was empty.

19

"I *knew* I should have brought an extra box," she said.

Liz stared longingly at the empty box. Then she looked out the window. The rain had let up, and mosquitoes were buzzing around the edge of the stream. We were so small that they looked like huge, stinging fighter planes. But that didn't stop Liz from watching them with hungry eyes.

"All right. I guess we can make a snack stop," the Friz decided.

She pressed a button on the dashboard and —

Pop! The Magic School Bus changed back to its normal size.

"Phew!" Arnold breathed a sigh of relief when he saw that the bus was on solid ground next to the stream. We were our normal size again, too. "I guess we're too heavy to float on the runoff now that we're big again," he said.

"Too bad," I said. "Getting washed away all the way down to the river would be great for my research."

But I knew that Liz really needed a

snack. She scooted outside the bus right away and began catching mosquitoes on her sticky tongue.

"Let's stay put, class," Ms. Frizzle suggested. "Liz won't take long."

Actually, the rest of us were pretty hungry, too. We were all glad when the Friz took a bunch of granola bars from the glove compartment and passed them around. As I ate, I looked at my library book.

"Uh-oh." Tim stopped in mid-crunch and stared out the bus windows. "Liz, be careful!" he called.

I looked out in time to see Liz climb onto a log at the edge of the stream.

"Oh, no!" I said. "The rough water could —"

Before I could finish, the rushing stream current pulled the log away from the stream bank. Liz scrambled to keep her balance.

"Liz is getting washed away!" cried Phoebe.

CHAPTER 3

We all jumped out of the Magic School Bus — but not fast enough. The stream whooshed Liz around a curve and out of sight.

"We have to do something!" I said.

We were all worried. Well, *almost* all of us.

"We'll catch up to Liz in no time," Ms. Frizzle said with a relaxed smile. "Back on the bus, everyone!"

Ms. Frizzle seemed pretty laid-back about Liz. I didn't get it. After all, Liz was just a little green lizard lost on a great rushing river. How could Ms. Frizzle be so sure we'd find her?

As soon as we were on board, the Friz started the engine and we were off — right *into* the stream.

Wanda gulped as the Magic School Bus was swept up in the fast current. "Well, D.A., it looks like you're getting your wish. We're getting washed away on this runaway water after all!"

"We're going to drown!" Arnold yelled.

He shouldn't have worried. Ms. Frizzle pressed a button on the dashboard and the bus began to change. The wheels puffed up to form a protective raft that stretched underneath and all around us. I don't know what happened to the top of the bus. Suddenly, it was just gone! I was glad to see the safety vests and helmets that appeared on top of our rain gear. We really needed them in that wild water.

"I guess going with the flow is one way to catch up to Liz," Carlos said. He grabbed the side of the raft as we surged forward. "Especially in this turbocharged stream!"

"Heavy rains *do* give streams extra

power," Ms. Frizzle agreed. "In fact, floods are the most deadly and damaging of all natural hazards in the United States."

A Flood Fact
by Wanda

Seven percent of the United States is prone to flooding. (That's an area about as big as the state of Texas!) However, less than one percent of the United States experiences severe floods. Floods cause about 125 deaths and billions of dollars of property damage every year.

"I just hope this strong current doesn't damage *Liz*," Ralphie said.

As we raced downstream, the Magic School Bus bounced past rocks and floating branches. It was awesome! The only bad part was that we didn't see any sign of Liz or the log she was on. And now it was starting to rain — again.

"This rain is definitely going to make it harder to take notes," I said.

"We've got bigger worries than that, D.A.," Wanda told me. "Did you see how high the water's getting? If this rain keeps up, the stream will overflow its banks!"

I shrugged. "According to my research, natural floodplains get floods fairly often. They happen along most streams about once every two years," I said. "They happen all over the country, too — in all 50 states."

"Is that supposed to make me feel better?" Arnold said, looking around nervously.

The stream we were on was getting a little wider, and then it emptied into a river. Even though the water had more room, all the rain was making it rush faster — and higher — than ever.

"A flood sure would be bad news for the buildings nearby," Ralphie said. He pointed at a farm that stood on one side of the river. We

saw another farm on the other side of the river, and even a factory.

"Why would anyone put buildings so close to a river that could flood?" Phoebe wondered. "If the water overflows, they could be destroyed!"

"People have lots of good reasons for living and working near rivers," Ms. Frizzle said. "Rivers provide water for farms, and for people and animals to drink. They're like highways, too. Businesses can use boats to bring in supplies and send things to other places."

I couldn't help but share what I had learned from my reading. "Rivers are sometimes used to make electricity," I added. "*And* rivers are fun for swimming and boating and waterskiing and stuff."

"You call *this* fun?" Arnold gaped up at the heavy rain that pelted down on us. "We're beyond wet!"

Arnold was right about that. We *were* beyond wet. We could find ourselves in the middle of a flood any minute, but I still wouldn't have wanted to be anywhere else.

"Uh-oh," said Carlos, peering ahead into the pouring rain. "Who put on the brakes?"

The river was slowing down — and so was the Magic School Bus. As soon as I looked downstream, I saw why. A bridge stretched over the river at a narrow point. Dozens of logs and branches were caught against the base of the bridge.

"It's a logjam," Keesha said. "Water can't get through."

"So that's why the river slowed down," I said. "How are we going to —"

Then I saw a flash of green scrambling over the logs right next to the bridge.

"Liz!" I yelled.

I was so happy to see her! We all shouted like crazy, but Liz didn't seem to hear us. I guess the heavy rain drowned out our voices.

"Oh, my gosh! Look how fast the water is rising!" said Phoebe.

I had been watching Liz, not the river. Now I saw that water was backing up because of the logjam.

"Uh-oh," I said. "I read about something like this in my book. When sticks, ice, or other things pile up in a river, they act like a dam. Water can't get through, so it backs up and causes a flood."

Water would flood up and over the bridge in no time! And then what would happen to Liz?!

CHAPTER 4

"Never fear," Ms. Frizzle said. "The Magic School Bus will break this up in a jiffy!"

She pressed a button on the dashboard. A bulldozer attachment grew from the front of our river raft.

Vrrrrooom!

The Friz revved the motor, and the Magic School Bus plowed right into the branches and logs.

Whoosh!

Water spilled through the opening our bulldozer had made. It gushed beneath the bridge in a torrent of white water, taking all the logs and branches with it.

"Hooray! We stopped the river from flooding!" Tim cheered. "Water's flowing under the bridge again."

"So is Liz!" I gasped.

Ahead of us, the rushing water swept Liz and her log out of sight beneath the bridge. *We* started moving fast again, too.

And that was a big problem.

"There's no room for the Magic School Bus to fit under the bridge!" Arnold cried. "The river is so high that we'll never get through!"

I couldn't believe it. We were about to smash right into the bridge!

"Never say never," Ms. Frizzle said.

She flipped a switch on the dashboard. In the next instant, the Magic School Bus changed into a submersible — with us inside. We dove right beneath the surface of the river.

Just in time.

"Luckily, some rivers run deep," the Friz told us. "And it's time we got to the *bottom* of this one."

"We never swam with fishes at my old school," said Phoebe.

"Forget about fishes. What about *Liz*?" Keesha said. "We can't just abandon her!"

"Oh, don't worry about Liz. She knows how to keep her head above water until we catch up with her," Ms. Frizzle said. "In the meantime . . ."

The Friz steered the Magic School Bus straight to the bottom of the river. It still seemed weird that she wasn't more worried about Liz. But we couldn't do anything about that, so we all looked out the bus windows.

At least, we *tried* to. The water was so cloudy and dirty that we couldn't see much.

"A river always carries dirt and plants and other debris in its current," the Friz explained. "When water overflows the riverbanks, some of that material is dumped on the nearby floodplain."

> ### There's Nothing Plain About a Floodplain!
> #### by Carlos
>
> A floodplain is the low, flat land on either side of a river, where water goes when the river overflows. The floodplain of the lower Mississippi River (the largest river in the United States) is more than 10 miles (16 km) across.

When we looked more closely, we could see what Ms. Frizzle was talking about. All around the Magic School Bus, sand and dirt and bits of plants dropped out of the muddy current and settled on the riverbed.

"I'm sure glad my house isn't on a flood-plain," said Wanda, crinkling up her nose. "I would *not* want a flooding river to dump all that junk in my yard."

Farmers Love Mud
by Ralphie

Floods deposit mud on the floodplain. The mud is rich in minerals and organic matter (bits of old plants and other growing things) that help crops to grow better. So it's not surprising that farmers have made use of the fertile floodplains for thousands of years.

In ancient Egypt, farmers waited until after the yearly flooding of the Nile River to plant their crops. The higher the floods, the better that year's crops were. Farmers even called the floods "the gift of the Nile."

"It may *look* like junk," said the Friz. "But the stuff deposited by rivers makes the floodplain soil perfect for growing things."

"So floods actually do good!" Keesha said. "Who would have guessed?"

"That's exactly why I thought we should get to the bottom of things," the Friz said. "I'm glad you now know that floods aren't all wet. They create healthy soil, too."

Just then, we splashed back to the surface with a pop.

Ralphie squinted into the rain. "Wow. It's just as wet *above* the water as it is below the surface," he said.

"Not to worry, class. We can still stay dry," said the Friz. She flipped a switch, and the Magic School Bus turned back into a river raft. This time, the raft came equipped with a roof.

"Great," I said. "Now my notebook won't get wet."

Still, I thought of someone who probably *was* wet, though. And she was certainly lost.

"I wish we could find Liz," Keesha said.

We peered into the sheets of rain. Ms. Frizzle had told us not to worry, but we couldn't help it! In all that frothy, white water we didn't see a single flash of lizard green.

We did see something else, though.

"Look at all those buildings," said Phoebe.

We were approaching a large town that sprawled out along one side of the river.

Houses and factories and warehouses were built right next to the water's edge.

"People need places to live and work," Ms. Frizzle said. "But building in areas that flood can be bad news."

Where Will Water Go?
by Phoebe

When plants and soil are covered up by buildings and parking lots, the ability of the land to soak up rainfall is reduced. That's because pavement and buildings can't absorb nearly as much water as plants and soil. That means a lot more water flows a lot more quickly into streams and rivers. More water makes floods more likely.

Tim frowned, looking ahead at the big town. "With all these buildings, most of the rainwater won't be able to soak into the earth," he said. "That means more runoff is flowing into the river and making it rise faster."

Things were getting serious. I guess maybe I should have been worried, but I was too busy taking notes on how fast the river was moving and how high it was getting! The water was so close to the top of the banks that people were piling up sandbags to keep the river from overflowing into the town.

"People here are doing a great job of pulling together to guard their town against a flood," Ms. Frizzle told us. "With enough warning, they can usually protect property and make sure everyone stays safe."

Ms. Frizzle pointed to a newspaper office building that stood next to the river. An electronic headline flashed across the outside wall: FLOOD WATCH IN EFFECT.

"At least it's just a flood *watch,* and not a flood *warning,*" Arnold said. "People here can work on that sandbag wall without worrying that they'll get washed away. At least, not yet."

Sounding the Alert
by Arnold

When people know about floods ahead of time, there's less chance that they or their property will be hurt or damaged. That's why the National Weather Service broadcasts warnings when a river or ocean is likely to flood.

A flood watch is issued when a flood may happen soon. You should prepare for a flood and stay tuned to the radio or television for more information.

A flood warning is issued when a flood is happening or will probably happen very soon. You may be advised to leave the area.

A flash flood warning is issued when a flash flood is happening. Anyone in the area should seek high ground right away.

It was inspiring to see so many people helping out. We even spotted a creature near the sandbags that *wasn't* a person.

It was Liz!

"We're here to rescue you!" Ralphie called out.

Liz just stood still on a sandbag and stared at us. Talk about weird. I mean, if I had been swept away by a river, you can bet I'd come rushing back to the Magic School Bus as soon as I could.

Not Liz! She just turned her back on the bus, scrambled over some sandbags, and disappeared from sight.

CHAPTER 5

"Did Liz just run away from us?" Keesha asked.

It wasn't the kind of question I could answer from my research. I couldn't figure out what was going on with Liz!

We all scanned the warehouses and factories that were right behind the sandbags. All of us except Ms. Frizzle, that is.

"Oh, Liz will find her way back to us," the Friz told us.

Huh? How could Ms. Frizzle be so sure? Instead of looking for Liz, the Friz just smiled and said, "Anyway, I think these workers could use some extra hands on the job. Don't you?"

A line of people hauled sandbags from a truck parked a hundred feet away. They all had red, sweaty faces and looked tired, but no one stopped. They couldn't afford to! The water was already almost up to the sandbags, and it was *still* raining.

"Let's do it!" we all said.

Ms. Frizzle steered the Magic School Bus to the edge of the river. She pressed a button, and our river raft turned back into a bus. All the people around us were so busy that they didn't seem to notice when the Friz steered the bus right out of the river.

"Hmm," I said. "What's that smell?"

As we got off the bus, I caught a whiff of . . . Well, I couldn't tell what it was, but there was something familiar about it.

Not that I had time to follow my nose. I was too busy! We joined the line of workers and started hoisting sandbags right away. It was hard work, but we were glad to help.

"Protecting cities and towns and farms from floods is a big job," Ms. Frizzle told us.

"Definitely," I said. I couldn't stop working to open up my book, but I didn't need to. I had already practically memorized the whole thing.

"Piling up sandbags is one way of keeping floodwaters back," I said. "But there are lots of others, too."

"You get my drift, D.A.!" said the Friz. "Levees, floodways, dams, and other structures really help to hold back floods."

"But . . . what if all that stuff *still* doesn't do the job?" Tim wondered. "I mean, if it rains enough, water could still overflow a levee *or* a sandbag wall, right?"

We all knew why he asked that question. The river was rising higher by the minute. The way it was raining, the water would reach the top of our sandbags in no time!

"Mother Nature has a way of getting past even the best human-made barriers," Ms. Frizzle admitted. "That's why it's important to keep informed."

Stop That Flood!

by D.A.

Human-made structures can do a lot to keep rivers from flooding.

- A **levee** is a wall that's built along the side  of a river, higher than the river's natural bank. A levee allows a river channel to carry more water.

- A **floodway** is a channel used for diverting floodwater. When water flows into a floodway, the water level in the main river goes down.

- A **dam** is a barrier built across a river to control the flow of water. During heavy rain, dams keep water from rushing downriver where it could cause floods. During dry weather, water is allowed to flow through the dam so areas downriver have water.

"I read all about forecasting," I said. "As soon as hydrologists get all that information, they use it to predict when a river will overflow — and when the water level will go back down to within its banks."

"So, if a river is going to overflow," Wanda said, "the National Weather Service gives information about when it will happen and how bad it will be. That way people have enough time to get to safety."

"And to protect their property," Phoebe added.

I guess the woman in front of us heard us talking. She turned around and said, "The last time the river flooded, I left my lawn furniture out and it ended up six blocks away! I won't make *that* mistake again."

I took another look at the rising river. "What about *this* time? Did the Weather Service predict when the river would overflow?" I asked the woman.

She moved another sandbag along the line. "They said this morning that the river would overflow tonight," she answered. "But this rain came sooner than we expected. If you ask me, we'll see the flood before that."

"Before?" Arnold squeaked out. His face was a pale, pasty white. "Can't we go back to school now?"

"And miss everything?" I said. "No way!"

Everyone hurried to pile more sandbags on top of the sandbag wall. We worked really fast, but the storm worked even faster!

Before we knew it, the river reached more than halfway up the sandbags. No one was surprised when a couple of police officers in storm gear showed up and told everyone to leave.

"Get out now!" one of the officers shouted through the pounding rain. "The river could overflow any minute. Everyone should move to higher ground."

"What about Liz?" Ralphie asked.

"She'll be all right," Ms. Frizzle reassured us. She waved us onto the Magic School Bus, but I couldn't help lingering behind.

Getting the Word Out

by Tim

The National Weather Service has a flood forecasting office in every state. Hydrologists (scientists who study water) there and at the United States Geological Survey do important work:

- They keep track of water conditions at river stations located along big rivers and on small streams near cities where floods occur.

- They measure how deep the water is, how fast it's flowing, and how much water flows past a particular point in a certain amount of time.

- They get reports on weather conditions and forecasts from meteorologists (scientists who study weather) in areas where floods occur.

- They use computer programs to predict how and when weather and water conditions will affect the river.

"Can't we look for just a minute?" I asked, scanning the warehouses and other buildings next to the river. "Maybe Liz is —"

I heard a loud whoosh of water.

"The river — it's flooding over the sandbags!" called Carlos. "Get on the bus *now*!"

I ran for the bus door, but I was too late. A wall of water swelled up behind me. It was taller than I was, and it was moving fast!

Wham! The water slammed into me, knocking me right off my feet.

"Hey!" I cried, but I couldn't do anything to stop it. Like a mighty sea giant, the floodwater snatched me up and sent me hurtling into the town.

Flood Power
by Arnold

As little as 6 inches (15 cm) of fast-moving water can knock a person off his or her feet. A car can be swept away in just 2 feet (61 cm) of moving water.

CHAPTER 6

"Whooooa!" I cried.

Water swirled everywhere around me. Being in it was like being in a turbocharged water ride! I didn't know which way was up.

The flood sent me flying past buildings and lampposts. It smacked into cars and fences, picking them up as if they were matchsticks. Even with my safety vest on, I had to be careful to steer clear of trees and signs and floating cars.

I tried to look everywhere at once. Talk about an exciting way to do research! I didn't want to miss a thing, but I started to realize how dangerous floods can be.

The roaring sounds of the rushing flood filled my ears. Then, as I whooshed past the windows of a brick factory building, I heard something else.

"Voices?" I said.

I pushed against the current, trying to turn around. Over my shoulder, I caught a glimpse of some people inside the factory. People — *and* a green lizard!

"Liz!" I shouted.

At least, I *thought* it was Liz. But then a forceful rush of the water carried me out of sight before I could be sure. With that flood crashing and swirling around me, I couldn't keep track of where the building was. Or where *I* was going!

At last, I saw a maple tree sticking out of the water. The trunk was mostly underwater, but a thick branch stuck out just above the surface. I made a grab for it and hung on tight. Somehow, I managed to climb up above the water. I couldn't believe how exhausted I was. I turned to look around, and the first thing I saw was . . .

"The Magic School Bus!" I tried to yell, but my voice was weak.

The bus had changed into a rescue boat. Ms. Frizzle was at the helm, and the rest of the class sat beneath the roof.

"D.A., you should never fear," the Friz said. "The Magic School Bus rescue squad is always near!"

The floodwater was still moving pretty fast. I don't know how Ms. Frizzle did it, but she managed to keep the Magic School Rescue Boat in one place while I climbed aboard. The Friz wrapped a blanket around me, gave me some hot chocolate, and made sure I didn't have hypothermia — a condition where your body temperature drops dangerously below normal. After Ms. Frizzle announced I would be OK, I remembered the factory.

"You'll never guess who I saw," I said. "Liz!"

I told them about the factory building and about the other people in there with her. "I'm pretty sure they're all trapped inside," I said.

"They're not the only ones in trouble," Tim said. "Look around!"

I hadn't *stopped* looking around. What I saw was totally unbelievable!

Floodwater reached halfway up the first floor of all the buildings. Rushing water piled cars on top of one another against a big government building. It knocked down lampposts and electric lines. Water sped by an overpass with so much force that part of the concrete crumbled into the water right before our eyes. Many of the buildings were empty, but not all of them. People crowded at some upper-floor windows — and even on the roofs.

"Wow!" I took out my notebook and began writing down everything I saw. "I guess the flood took some people by surprise, since it came earlier than the Weather Service said it would."

"It looks as if rescue workers were prepared, anyway," said Wanda. She pointed to a couple of rescue boats that appeared on the water. "Help is on the way!" one of the crew yelled through a bullhorn.

Boom!

A loud explosion made all of us jump right out of our seats.

"Part of that building just blew out!" Phoebe said.

She pointed at a paint supply warehouse near the river. Flames burst out of a jagged hole that had blown through the outside wall.

The Friz had to move fast to steer the

Magic School Rescue Boat away from the flames. "We'd better leave this to the professionals. Hazardous materials are serious stuff," she said. "It's good to see that no one was still in that building."

All kinds of debris floated around us. And there was lots of thick, gooey, *stinky* mud on everything. Just looking at it made my stomach churn.

From the Desk of Ms. Frizzle

When Do Fire and Water Mix?

Natural disasters such as floods and earthquakes can cause hazardous material spills. These materials cause extra dangers during floods. Gas, chlorine, or propane leaks can lead to explosions. Electric lines can snap and electrify water, metal — and people around them.

Too Much Water Won't Put Out a Fire
by Wanda

Floods make firefighters' hard jobs even harder. In 1997, residents of Grand Forks, North Dakota, saw four-foot floodwaters overtake their town. While the Red River raged out of control, one of the downtown buildings caught fire. Firefighters had trouble getting close to the burning building in the deep water, and their waterlogged equipment wouldn't work. The fire continued to spread. Luckily, a helicopter crew was able to drop flame-retardant chemicals to slow the blaze, but not all fire departments have access to helicopters and other specialized equipment.

Ralphie whistled, looking all around us. "Do *all* floods cause this much damage?" he asked.

"Some are even worse," I said. "In 1993, big flooding on the Mississippi River wrecked more than 40,000 buildings and killed almost 50 people. One of the country's worst floods hit in 1889. It was in Johnstown, Pennsylvania, and it was caused by a broken dam upriver. About 2,200 people were killed."

At least this flood didn't seem as destructive as some of the ones I had read about in my research. But seeing that big explosion and all that debris and rushing water made me worry even more about Liz.

I looked around, trying to find the factory where I'd spotted Liz. It wasn't easy with all that heavy rain and thick fog and mud. But at last I saw the big brick building.

"That's the place!" I said.

"Excellent work, D.A.!" said Ms. Frizzle. She steered the Magic School Rescue Boat toward the factory, but we didn't get very far. We'd only gone about a dozen yards when a deep voice boomed out over a megaphone.

"You, in that boat," the voice called. "Hold it right there!"

CHAPTER 7

"Stop? *Now?*" I said. "But we're so close to saving Liz!"

It wasn't as if we had a choice. Ms. Frizzle cut the motor of the boat.

A rescue raft floated on the flooded street about 20 feet behind us. Two people were in it. The foggy rain made them look like smudged shadows, but I was pretty sure they wore police uniforms. One of the officers held a megaphone.

"There's a group of preschoolers trapped inside a bus just west of here," he called through the rain. "Can you help with the rescue?"

I guess they couldn't see us clearly. They thought we were emergency rescue workers!

Helping Hands
by Keesha

When there are floods, lots of different people work together to rescue victims. Local police and fire departments are usually first on the scene. Specially trained flood rescue teams are usually called in, too. During bad floods, state police, the National Guard (a military group in each state that can be called on in emergencies), and even the U.S. Army send workers to help.

With so many people on the job, good communication is important. Managers use two-way radios to stay in constant contact so they can make sure workers go where they are needed most.

I still wanted to find Liz, but how could we say no? "This will be great for my research. Let's go!" I said.

"But we're just schoolkids," Phoebe said.

"Precisely!" said the Friz. "Learning is our biggest job — and helping those emergency workers is the perfect way to find out how flood victims are rescued."

She hit the gas and let out a wild shout. "Wahoo! Let's take chances! Get messy! And save those preschoolers!"

ATTENTION TEACHERS:

PLEASE DO *NOT* TRY THIS ON *YOUR* NEXT FIELD TRIP! DRIVING IN FLOODWATERS IS THE CAUSE OF ALMOST HALF OF ALL U.S. FLOOD DEATHS. UNLESS YOU HAVE A MAGIC SCHOOL BUS, YOU SHOULD NOT DRIVE IN A FLOOD.

The next thing we knew, Ms. Frizzle steered the Magic School Rescue Boat behind the officers' boat and . . .

"Check it out," said Tim. "We're changing!"

That was for sure. Our heads got pointy, like cones. When I looked down, I saw that the rest of my body looked like the body of a rubbery torpedo, with a handle on each side. Everyone else's did, too! We looked a lot like something I had seen in my book.

"We're rescue flotation devices!" I realized. I touched the rope that was tied to the pointy end of my head. "A rescue worker can throw us to the preschoolers' bus. That way the kids can hold on to us and stay above the water while they're being taken from the bus."

"Thanks for the science briefing, D.A.," Carlos said. "I guess being a cone head isn't *all* bad, since we can give flood victims something to hang on to."

"How true!" the Friz agreed.

"We can sure use the help," one of the rescue workers from the other boat called out. "This is the worst flood we've had around here in 15 years."

How Bad Is It?

by Arnold

Scientists use a rating system for floods that suggests how often a flood of that size occurs.

- A three-year flood is fairly common. The term "three-year flood" means there is a one-in-three chance of a stream flooding to that level in any year.

- A larger flood is less common. A flood that reaches a higher level might only happen once every 10 years. That flood would be called a 10-year flood.

- A flood so large that it occurs an average of just once every 100 years is called a 100-year flood.

Being part of an important rescue effort made my whole body buzz with excitement — my flotation-device body, that is. I saw that lots of other equipment was piled around us in the rescue boat, too. Safety vests, ropes, flares, whistles, two-way radios — you name it! It was definitely crowded in there.

Before long, we found our way to the bus of preschoolers. Talk about a serious situation! Floodwater had pushed the school bus off the road and against a tree. The bus was still right-side up — but just barely. Water surged all around it. The current was so strong that Ms. Frizzle couldn't get the Magic School Rescue Boat close to the busload of preschoolers.

"It's a good thing you're here," a rescue worker from the other boat called out. "Our raft's too small for all the kids. You've got a lot more space in your boat."

"Whatever I can do to help," the Friz yelled back. "What's the first step?"

"It's just too deep," the rescuer replied. "We'll have to help the kids across. We can tie a rope between your boat and the bus and use a harness and flotation devices to ferry the kids out."

"But . . ." Keesha bit her lip and stared nervously at the strong current. "How can we be sure everyone will stay safe?"

"Not to worry, Keesha," Ms. Frizzle said. "Rescue work is dangerous. But flood rescue workers get lots of special training."

Rescue Workers Get a Workout
by Ralphie

Flood rescue workers have to learn many different skills, such as:
- how to operate and handle a boat.
- water lifesaving techniques.
- first aid.
- rope rescue skills.
- animal rescue.
- how to handle hazardous materials.
- radio communication.
- search techniques.
- how to evacuate people in swiftly moving water.

"I'm glad they know what they're doing, because this is some seriously scary stuff," said Wanda.

Just watching them, it was pretty obvious that the rescue officers knew just what to do. Within minutes, they tied a long rope between the Magic School Rescue Boat and the bus of kids. One officer put on a safety harness, clipped it to the rope, and gave Ms. Frizzle a signal.

The Boy Who Was Caught in a Drain Pipe

by Wanda

Flood rescue teams face very challenging situations. One time, a boy was swept into a series of underground pipes while he played with his boogie board in a ditch. The boy became trapped in a narrow passageway under a storm drain. Luckily, rescue workers heard his cries for help. They used sandbags to block water so it wouldn't flood the culvert and drown the boy. Then, using heavy rescue equipment, they opened up the drain and got the boy out.

"All right!" the Friz said. "Let the rescue begin!"

The officers jumped into the water. One forced the bus door open and reached out to the child closest to him. The little boy took his hand and then grabbed onto a flotation device. That was Ralphie — he volunteered to go first. The officer held on to the boy and moved his way through the water by holding on to the rope. We all cheered when Ralphie and the preschooler arrived safely on the deck of the Magic School Rescue Boat.

The two officers took turns pulling themselves through the water along the rope. Every time one of them reached the school bus, Ms. Frizzle threw a flotation device over. In other words, she was throwing us across!

"I was never tossed into a raging flood at my old school," said Phoebe.

A second later, the Friz threw Phoebe across to the bus of preschoolers. Phoebe looked really nervous, but I was ready. I was more than ready! It was hard to stand by until my part of the rescue came.

At last, the Friz picked *me* up. "Whee!" I said as she launched me into the air.

It was amazing! Like taking a flying leap from a trampoline. As I sailed through the cool air, I caught a glimpse of the dark, swirling currents of water below. Then . . .

"Yes!" I crowed as one of the rescue workers caught me.

The next thing I knew, a little girl grabbed on tight to my handles. The rescue worker was leading her back through the water to the Magic School Rescue Boat, talking calmly to her the whole time.

Craaa-aaack!

A loud noise made me look up. I hadn't noticed that a large limb had splintered off the tree that the bus of preschoolers was leaning against. The branch must have cracked when the bus first banged into the tree. Now the weight of the branch was making it fall!

While I watched, the branch smashed into a power line — snapping it in two.

"Oh, no!" I gasped.

An electric buzz filled the air. The sound of it made me want to jump right out of my skin!

The loose ends of the power line sput-

tered with sparks. One end caught on the tree. That was great news because I knew wood doesn't conduct electricity.

But I also knew that water *does* conduct electricity, and that was just where the other end of the power line was headed. It swung down through the air past the tree — straight toward the rescue worker, the little girl, and me.

CHAPTER 8

I love to see science in action. But this was too much — even for me!

"We're going to be fried!" I shouted.

I gaped up at the power line — and then blinked in total surprise.

I thought I saw something green and lizardlike sitting on the tree right next to the falling wire.

"Liz?" I wondered aloud.

Sure, there was foggy rain all around. But I thought it *had* to be Liz. Didn't it?

In a flash, a thin green arm reached out with a branch. The branch hit the power line and changed its direction. Instead of falling

73

down to zap us, the power line caught on another branch and was left dangling in the air.

Phew! I had never felt so relieved in my life. The rescue worker, the little girl, and I made it to the Magic School Rescue Boat without getting hurt.

Phoebe's Word of Advice

Never, never, never go near a power line that's down. Let experts (and magic lizards) handle such deadly situations.

"Did you see that?" I said to the rest of the class. "Liz saved us! She was up in the tree. She is the smartest lizard ever! She knew to use a branch to move that electrical wire since wood doesn't conduct electricity. Didn't you see her?"

I looked back up at the tree, but you know what? Liz was gone!

Ralphie blinked up into the rain-drenched branches. "Are you sure you saw right?" he asked me. "I mean, maybe being a flotation device affected your eyesight, D.A."

Then the other rescue worker called over from the other boat, "Hey! Did anyone see that lizard?" He pointed up at the branch where I'd seen Liz. "It reached out with a stick and . . ."

Then he stopped talking and shook his head. "Nah, it couldn't be," he said. "The stress of this rescue must be getting to me."

"See? Liz *was* there, I know it!" I said.

The trouble was, Liz wasn't in the tree anymore. And we didn't have a clue to where she could have gone.

We all kept our eyes open while the Magic School Rescue Boat and the other rescue boat carried the preschoolers away from their bus on the flooded streets. We didn't see Liz. But we did see other rescue workers helping people who were trapped in buildings, trees — even on the roofs of some mobile homes.

Finally, we reached higher ground. Two big buses were parked there, a safe distance from the water.

"One of those buses will take these pre-schoolers and their teachers to a shelter," Ms. Frizzle said as she helped the little kids out of the Magic School Rescue Boat. "Emergency workers there will contact the kids' families so they'll know their children are safe and are waiting to be picked up once their parents can get there safely."

After all the kids were on the bus, the guys in the other rescue boat steered back

across the floodwaters to look for other people who needed help.

Lots of Helping Hands
by Phoebe

When floods strike, people everywhere join forces to help.

• Groups like the Red Cross and the Salvation Army provide shelter, food, and medical services to flood victims and to rescue workers.

• Private companies and volunteer groups donate food, water, blankets, towels, heaters, toothbrushes, and lots of other things needed by people who have been flooded out of their homes. Businesses donate tools and supplies for cleaning up, repairing, and rebuilding after a flood.

"Whoa!" Phoebe said as we all returned to our normal selves and tumbled out of the pile of flotation devices in the back of the boat.

"We were never packed like sardines at my old school."

We were all dripping wet — and cold, too, from being in that water. But it was worth it.

"At least we got to help some kids in need," I said. "*And* we soaked up some great information on floods!"

Still, it felt good to be my old self again. The rain was letting up, too, and the fog was lifting.

"Maybe we'll be able to find Liz now," Keesha said, peering into a flooded alleyway between two buildings.

For the next two hours, we puttered all over the floodwaters in our raft. We looked for Liz inside cars that had been flipped upside down. We called into flooded houses and stores. We looked up into trees and on top of roofs. We tried to go back to the factory where I'd spotted Liz, but we couldn't get near it because a gas line had exploded nearby.

"What are we going to do now?" Tim asked.

Usually, when I want to know something, I just read about it in one of my books. But I had a feeling that not even a book about lizards — or one about floods — would help us this time.

I was starting to wonder if we would *ever* find Liz.

CHAPTER 9

Everyone in our class really wanted to keep looking for Liz. We would have, too. Except for one thing.

"You there!" a man called out from a rescue boat. Sitting next to him was a woman. They both wore military uniforms.

"Don't tell me we're going to be dragged into *another* rescue operation," Arnold said.

I wouldn't have minded — not a bit! But we didn't get the chance. Now that the rain and fog were clearing, the rescue workers saw right away that we were kids. Let me tell you, they did *not* look happy about it.

"Don't you know it's dangerous out here?"

the woman said. "These waters can be treacherous, even for trained rescue teams. You need to get to safe, high ground right away."

We tried to tell them about Liz, but it was no use. The rescue workers made us follow them to the same place where we had taken the preschoolers we had helped rescue earlier.

"That bus will take you to a shelter where you can get food and water," the woman told us, pointing to a yellow bus that sat at the top of the hillside.

"Thanks, but I don't think we'll have trouble getting a ride," said Wanda.

The rescue workers looked puzzled to hear that, but I knew exactly what Wanda was talking about. As soon as the other boat was out of sight, the Friz pressed a button next to the steering wheel of the rescue boat. Right away, our boat sprouted wheels.

"We're back on the bus!" Carlos said.

"Yeah, but . . ." Keesha frowned as Ms. Frizzle steered the Magic School Bus past the other bus at the top of the hill. "I feel sorry for the people who had to leave their homes and

businesses. With all this flooding, it will probably be a while before they can go back."

"Getting things back in shape after a flood is a big job," Ms. Frizzle agreed.

"I guess that's why people are always trying to think of better ways to guard against floods," Tim said.

"Not just with human-made barriers like levees, either," I agreed. "I read in my book about how towns are taking steps to build up the land's *natural* defenses against floods."

Treating the Floodplain
by Ralphie

In areas where floods occur, people often take steps to treat floodplains so they can soak up more rainfall.

- Many towns have passed laws to limit development near rivers.

- Wetlands are especially good at absorbing water. That's one reason why governments are taking steps to preserve and restore wetlands and save them from development.

- Planting trees and plants on floodplains helps to control erosion (when soil is washed away by rain) and increase absorption.

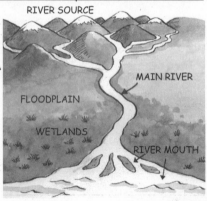

RIVER SOURCE

MAIN RIVER

FLOODPLAIN

WETLANDS

RIVER MOUTH

"But it seems like rivers are bound to overflow sometimes, no matter what," Ralphie said.

The Friz nodded. "That's why some towns are taking even stronger steps. They're trying to convince people that they'll be better off if they *leave* the floodplain."

"That's right," I chimed in. "Some local governments give tax breaks and special loans to people who move out of areas that flood. Sometimes the government even buys up properties so they can turn parts of the floodplain into grassy parks that are better at soaking up heavy rains."

I didn't know if there were any plans like that in the town we were in, but I *did* know that *lots* of people had been flooded out of their houses and businesses. We got to meet some of them ourselves after the Friz drove the Magic School Bus to a school that had been turned into a temporary shelter.

Talk about busy. That place was hopping! Cots filled the whole gym, and people whose homes had been flooded were camped there.

Flood Recovery Doesn't Happen in a Day

by D.A

It can take months – or even years – for towns to recover from floods. Here's why:

- Governments have to fix or replace damaged structures such as roads, bridges, levees, water and sewage treatment plants, power facilities, and other things that towns really depend on.

- Mud and water from floods can be contaminated by sewage and other hazardous materials that may have leaked. Flooded buildings must be dried out, cleaned up, and disinfected.

- Businesses may have to repair or replace expensive machinery and equipment.

- Connections to appliances must be checked before gas, oil, and electrical service is restored.

A medical center was set up in the auditorium. Signs pointed the way to bathrooms and showers. Tables were piled high with food, drinking water, blankets, towels, clothes, soap, toothbrushes — you name it! And people were coming all the time with more supplies.

"All these volunteers are here to make sure people who had to evacuate have all the help they need," Ms. Frizzle said.

"Here comes another busload," we heard one of the volunteers say. "A group of factory workers was caught inside the Acme Pet Food building when the water crested."

A dozen wet, mud-covered people tromped into the shelter. The last person started to let the door shut behind her. Just before it closed, a small green lizard scuttled through the opening.

"Liz!" we all cried.

This time Liz didn't run away. She scampered right over to us, and the Friz picked her up. I'm not sure how you can tell when a lizard is smiling. But I know Liz was smiling then. All of us kids were, that's for sure! So was Ms. Frizzle.

"Hey, Lou, there's that lizard we saw in the factory," one of the workers said to another. "I guess it hitched a ride in our rescue boat."

The worker named Lou smiled at Liz, then said to Ms. Frizzle, "I'm glad you got your lizard back, ma'am. I don't know how it got into the factory, but I couldn't resist feeding it a couple handfuls of Lucky Lizard Lumps while we waited for the rescue team. I hope you don't mind."

"Lucky Lizard Lumps?" Phoebe said. "Hey, D.A.! That factory where you saw Liz must have been the Acme Pet Food factory!"

I nodded. "Remember that weird smell near the sandbags? No wonder it seemed familiar — it was Lucky Lizard Lumps! Liz must have caught a whiff of it. That's why she ran away from us. She was looking for lunch!"

We were really glad that mystery was solved. But there was still something I was puzzled about.

"If Liz was in the factory, do you really think she could have swatted that electrical wire away so it wouldn't zap us?" I asked.

"Get real, D.A.," Ralphie told me. "I mean, how could a lizard get from the factory all the way across town in a raging flood?"

If Liz knew the answer to Ralphie's question, she sure wasn't telling. But you know what? When we all climbed back on the Magic School Bus a while later, I could have sworn I saw Liz and Ms. Frizzle wink at each other.

D.A.'s Flood Safety Tips

If a flood is expected in your area, be sure to:

- Keep a battery-operated radio on hand for storm information (in case the electricity goes out).
- Fill bathtubs and sinks with water, in case drinking water becomes contaminated. Floods can cause sewers to back up into the water supply.
- Bring outdoor furniture inside.
- Move valuable items to upper floors.
- Plan and practice an evacuation route. Be prepared to evacuate if advised by police or emergency workers.
- Turn off electricity and gas, if advised.
- Put your pets on a leash or in a carrying case, so you can evacuate them with you.